Ruffles
goes to school

by Angela King

MHP

Moat House Publishing
London, United Kingdom

Published by
Moat House Publishing Ltd.

Copyright © Angela King 2022
All rights reserved.

Angela King has asserted her right under the Copyright, Designs and Patents Act 1988
to be identified as the author of this work.

This book is sold subject to the condition that it shall not, by way of trade
or otherwise, be photocopied, lent, hired out, resold or otherwise circulated without
Moat House Publishing Ltd's prior consent
in any form of binding or cover other than that in which it is published
and without a similar condition, including this condition, being imposed
on the subsequent purchaser.

ISBN 978-1-8383174-3-0

First published in Great Britain in 2022
by Moat House Publishing Ltd.

Contents artwork © Moat House Publishing Ltd.

For Bradley.

May you always be surrounded by love.

On their first day at school,
the children stood in the yard.

For some it was easy,
for some it was hard.

A long, tall boy bent his knees to look smaller.

A little girl jumped on a step to look taller.

A boy pulled his hat over his golden, curly hair.

A girl started singing; she loved them all to stare!

A big, round boy kept his coat buttoned tight.

Sue put her glasses in her pocket, out of sight.

They moved slowly to the classroom,
each wanting to go home.

Their little voices silent,
trying hard not to moan.

The teacher looked around the room,
then told them all, 'sit down.'

She opened her book,
she had a look,
and then began to frown.

'Two children are not here yet!'
She jumped up from her chair.

'Today is their first day at school,
I don't know
how they dare.'

The teacher hopped on one foot,
then ran out of the room.

She shouted from the corridor.

'I will come back soon!'

Just outside the window,
two children stood quite still.

One was Ruffles – a furry child,
the other was little Bill.

Little Bill was crying,
not knowing what to do.

Ruffles held his tiny hand.
'I will look after you.'

The teacher clapped her hands twice.

'Hurry, you are late!'

She watched them go into the class,
then went to shut the gate.

The children started pointing,
their mouths dropped open wide.

The moment they saw Ruffles,
their shock they could not hide.

'Why are you covered in fur?'
'Why is your fur blue?'
'Are you a boy?'
'Are you a girl?'

They didn't
have
a clue.

Ruffles sighed and bowed his head;
he then looked up to speak.

'I do not know;
I cannot give the answers that you seek.'

The teacher gave them pencils,
paper and some paint.

'Amuse yourselves, I need a break,
some tea before I faint.'

The teacher left the classroom,
the children raised a smile...

Oh, what teasing they could do,
if she was gone a while.

The day dragged on for Ruffles,
he ran home after school.

He cried out to his furry mum,
'The children have been cruel.'

His mum hugged him tightly,
his tears began to flow.

'I will tell you my own story, Son,
from many years ago.'

'I was once a child myself – mocking did occur.

One night I asked my own mum to cut off all my fur.

She did as I had asked her, but she already knew...

Under all my curly fur, my skin was also blue!

I looked into the mirror,
at a face I'd never seen...

My wonky ears,
my strange black nose,
I gave out
a little scream!'

'Sometimes things are hurtful, Son,
and sometimes things are good.

Some people have things they
would change,
if only they just could.

But please remember this, my child,
you are who you are.

Be happy in your own skin,
and it will take you far.

Work with what you have, Son,
help others do it too.

The world has many shapes and colours
– yours is furry blue.

So, kindness is the answer,
be gentle on yourself.

And then be kind to others,
they might need it for their
health!'

Ruffles went to bed that night,
then sneaked back down the stairs.

He took the scissors from the drawer,
and cut off all his hairs.

He stared into the mirror,
only to discover...

He also had a wonky ear,
much bigger than the other!

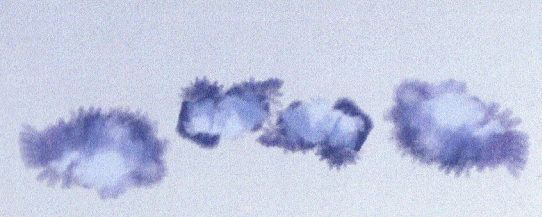
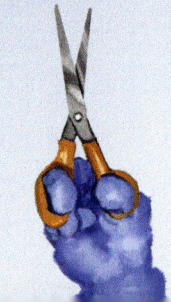

The next morning rather early,
Ruffles went to school.

He wore a hood, he wore a scarf,
he felt like such a fool.

The others did not notice,
they were teasing one and all;
Shouting out that one was big,
one was clumsy,
one was small.

Ruffles did not like this,
he remembered what Mum had said.

He decided at that moment,
to be himself instead.

The teacher clapped her hands.
'Just amuse yourselves today.

I really need my tea break,
so go ahead and play.'

She pointed over to Ruffles.

'What is that creature at the back?'

The children screamed and stood on chairs; in case it might attack!

Ruffles threw off his hood and scarf,
then walked up to the teacher.

'Hello, it's still me, Ruffles,
I'm very pleased to meet ya!'

The teacher raised
her eyebrows,

'A brave child, now I see.'

Ruffles smiled, he felt so proud.
'There's nobody quite like me!"

If we are going to play a game,
I ask if we all could...

Take turns at saying something nice,
I really think we should.'

The children clapped,
then little Bill stood up
without a fear.

'Ruffles is a lovely child,
it's good to have him here.'

'Please put on your glasses.'

Two girls called out to Sue.

'Then you will see us waving,
we want to be friends with you.'

The round boy
stood up boldly,
he sang a song in tune.

A certain girl
was happy.
'Let's sing together soon.'

A girl looked at the tall boy,
his face he'd painted green.

She said,
'You have the sweetest smile
that I have ever seen.'

The day was filled with lots of fun,
and what they came to know...

With respect, care and kindness,
friendships could grow and grow.

Books by Angela King

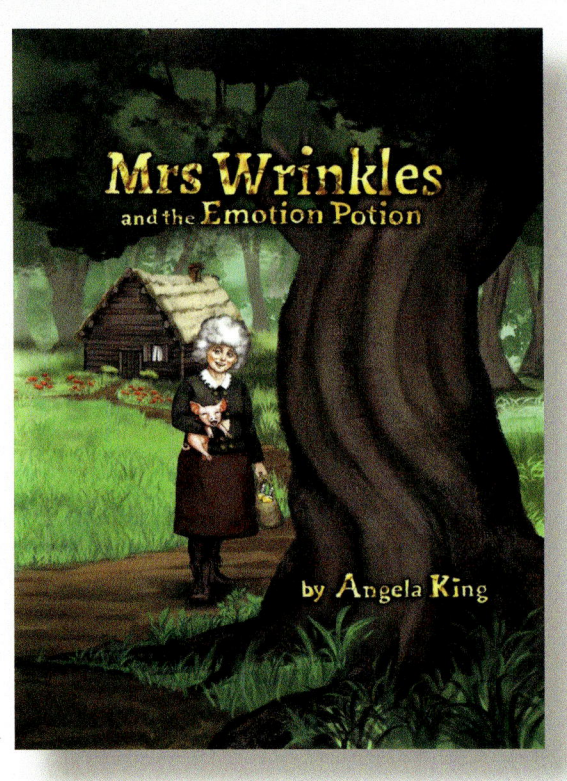 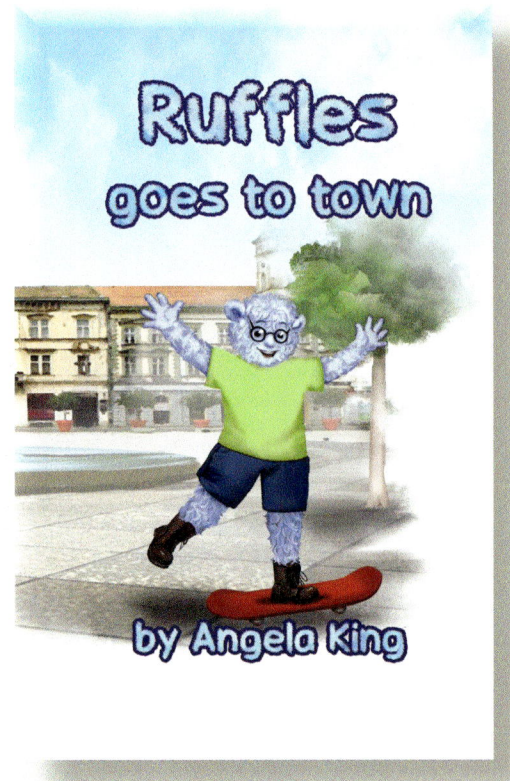